VIRAL

THE RISE AND FALL OF A NATION

DOZER MILLON JR

Copyright © 2023 Dozer Millon Jr.

All rights reserved.

ISBN: 9798863113906

The story, all names, characters, and incidents portrayed in this work are fictitious. No identification with actual persons (living or deceased), places, buildings, and products is intended or should be inferred.
dozermillonjr@gmail.com

CHAPTER 1

Asiya slowly opens her eyes to find herself trapped in rubble. She screams for help, but she can barely hear her own voice, drowned by the ringing in her ears. As the dust begins to settle, Asiya's senses return to her. She coughs and sputters as she struggles to breathe through the thick dust that fills the air. A heavy beam pins her legs down and she could not move them.

"Help!" she screams, her voice hoarse and weak. "Can anyone hear me?"

There was no response. Asiya begins to feel a sense of hopelessness. But she refuses to give up. She pushes against the beam with all her might, but it wouldn't budge.

And then, she hears a faint sound. It was a shuffling noise, like someone moving debris.

"Hello?" she calls out, her voice barely above a whisper.

There was a pause, and then she hears footsteps approaching.

"Is anyone there?" she calls out again.

And then she sees him. A man emerges from the rubble, dressed in tattered clothes and covered in dust.

"Thank God you're here," she says. A sense of relief

washes over her.

The man approaches and kneels down beside her. "Are you okay?" he asks.

Asiya shakes her head. "I can't move. My legs are trapped."

The man assesses the situation. He begins to clear the debris, being careful not to cause further harm, until he sees the beam trapping Asiya's legs.

"Can you move your legs?" he asks.

Asiya tries, but the pain was too much. "No," she says, tears rolling down her face.

"I will try to lift the beam then, on my cue, you try to slide out." says the man.

Asiya nods.

"Ready…," he said. "Now!"

Asiya gasps as she feels the weight lifted from her legs. She tries to move them and—to her relief—finds that she could. She immediately pulls her legs away from under the beam then starts sliding out from the rubble.

"Thank you," she says, her voice trembling with emotion.

The man smiles, then helps her to her feet. "Come on," he said. "Let's get you away from here."

Still dazed and disoriented, Asiya sits on the metal bench near a broken vending machine and begins to reflect on the near-death experience she had just had. She recalls arriving to work before dawn, which she really enjoys. Then, as she entered the building, there was a loud bang, and everything went dark. She now finds herself staring at the mezzanine floor above, through the gaping hole from the collapsed ceiling—furniture, medical and research appliances scattered wherever she looks.

Asiya feels a tap on her shoulder. It was the man who saved her, holding a bottle of water. "Here, you need this," he says, handing her the bottle.

Asiya takes it and smiles. "Thank you," she says, then begins to take a sip.

She did not realize how parched she was until what started as a sip had turned into guzzling, as she downs the bottle the man just gave her. The feeling of the water rushing down her throat starts to relax her and makes her feel less frazzled.

As she looks at him to say thanks once again, she suddenly notices something, the guy looks very familiar—the smile, the wince, and especially the crinkling of the nose. It is as if she knows him from a past life.

"Have we met?" Asiya asks.

"I don't think so," the man replies. "Trust me, I would certainly remember if I met you," he continues, as he lowers his backpack to the ground, takes a knee and starts rustling through his stuff to find his phone.

Her eyes continue to survey him, particularly his face, as she struggles to figure out where she might have seen him—Could he be a distant relative? A childhood neighbor perhaps? Maybe an old acquaintance? Then, she notices the blood that's been creeping down the man's face.

"You're bleeding." she utters. "Are you alright?"

Before the man could answer, she presses on with a series of questions. The fuss in her tone is noticeable. "How did you get injured? Any headache, dizziness, or confusion? Any sensitivity to noise or light, changes in hearing or vision?"

Unsure of how to react to the battery of questions, he decides to take a dig at her. "Well, I didn't have any of those until about a second or two ago," he said, clearly trying very hard to contain himself from bursting into laughter. "I am beginning to hear ringing in my ears now and my vision is beginning to blur," continued the man, eyes welling up in tears amid the struggle to contain his laughter.

Embarrassed, Asiya, with puckered lower lip and drooped eyebrows, muttered, "I'm sorry. It's a reflex."

They both break into a fit of laughter.

"Thank you. I needed that." says Asiya. "I am not sure if I already did, but thank you again for saving my life." she continues. "By the way, my name's Asiya. I am a researcher here. I am a doctor, and it would really make me feel better if you'd let me look at that wound. It's the least I can do after what you've done."

"Alright doc. Thank you," says the man. "Call me Nasir."

"Hello Nasir," says Asiya as she goes into the nearby room to get medical supplies.

Nasir acknowledges with a nod.

Asiya comes out with a tray of medical supplies. She starts donning a pair of medical gloves and begins to examine Nasir's wound.

"It's not deep, but I still have to clean it properly to avoid infection. This might sting a bit," Asiya says, as she begins to debride the wound.

Bzzt— Bzzt— Bzzt— Nasir's phone vibrates, followed by a chime, just as Asiya finishes bandaging the wound. While Nasir takes out the phone from his pocket to check the message, an intrigued and curious Asiya positions herself—without being overly obvious—to get a glimpse of the message. She succeeds. She could not, however, completely make out what it means. The message reads:

"Namir, stem cells are activated. [pinned location]."

Nasir hurriedly picks up his bag, slings one strap on to his shoulder and grabs Asiya by the arm. "We have to go!" he exclaims, then pulls Asiya through the corridor and onto the fire exit.

"What's going on?!" Asiya asks as she tries to keep up with the pace.

"Something tells me this is not a random event," says Nasir as they make their way to the podium level above.

As they exit through the door leading to the podium deck, a grim sight welcomes them—pockets of black smoke billowing all around the city. At the end of the podium deck is a crashed AeVTOL military cargo pod—

an autonomous electric vehicle capable of vertical take-off and landing. The crashed pod has gone all the way inside the building's mezzanine floor. Down the road, onlookers begin to form a crowd around the building. There are no signs of any first responder.

Nasir heads to the pod to investigate. Asiya follows. Nasir takes out a handheld device about the size of an oversized phone, only a lot thicker, from his bag. He starts tapping on the device until a wide beam of red light comes out. He then begins moving around the pod and scanning it. As they approach the other side, they see the pod's door completely detached from its fuselage—inside, Asiya immediately recognizes the cargo.

"That's the vaccine we just developed!" Asiya exclaimed, as she looked at the dripping boxes and broken vials of serum scattered inside the hull. "This is the first batch that is scheduled for transport today."

"Well, it appears someone tried to hijack it." Nasir said, referring to the report from his scanner. He then begins to explain.

"I am an officer in the UAE Special Operations Command. Two days ago, we received an intel from the State Security Department about a threat of multiple attacks around the city planned today. I was sent here as part of a supplementary patrol in response to that threat. When I arrived, I saw the pod taking off erratically and then crash landed into the building. I immediately went inside to see if anyone needed any help and that's when I heard you."

"I thought you were also a doctor or a researcher. I caught a glimpse of the message you received earlier saying something about activated stem cells," Asiya says.

Nasir explains, "The 'stem cells' refer to a group of agents, similar in concept to terrorist 'sleeper cells', except it has a positive goal—to repair the society, much like how stem cells repair a broken body, in the event of a major crisis. That earlier message indicates we are in the middle of a crisis of such magnitude."

He further explains a directive called the 'Aistimraria Protocol'—a government directive responsible for activating the 'stem cells'. But before he could go deeper, they hear a commotion from down the road. They look over and see the crowd down the building screaming and scrambling away from an oncoming team of six heavily-armed men in black uniform.

"En route to eliminate the target!" they hear the leader say, followed by "Go! Go! Go!" as the team rushes towards the entrance to the left side of the building. They hear a loud bang as the men breach the door.

"We need to go!" exclaims Nasir. "I do not know what they're here for and I am not staying to find out!" he continues.

"I know a quick way to the other side of the building. Follow me!" said Asiya.

Asiya leads Nasir to a door secured by a security console. Asiya looks into the device and the door opens to a tight corridor with different laboratory setups on each side. They run down the corridor and exit to the west side of the building. From there they go in and down the fire exit to get to the main street—where they blend in with the fleeing crowd and make their way towards the corner.

As they turn right at the bend, Nasir takes out his car keys and presses the remote. The headlights of a white Nissan Patrol flash twice just a few meters in front of them, followed by a purring from its massive 5.6L engine. They both enter the car, hurriedly slam the doors and immediately buckle up. Nasir plugs in his phone in the center console.

"Computer, check the last message on my phone with attached pin location and set course to it," says Nasir.

"Got it!" said a synthetic voice coming out the dashboard speakers. "Found message with last pinned location. Setting course now." The voice then continues, "Unassisted driving commencing in 3... 2... 1..."

"We should be safe now," says Nasir, as the SUV moves out from the roadside parking.

The morning daylight begins to break as they join the main road on the way to the pinned location.

CHAPTER 2

The stage was set with a grand podium adorned with a large emblem made up of the letters, 'CDPC'. The room was filled with important scientists, researchers, and other notable people from the world of medicine. The excitement was palpable as the attendees eagerly awaited the start of the evening's affair—today the UAE Centre for Disease Prevention and Control is set to announce a breakthrough in the fight against the ongoing pandemic.

As the lights dimmed, a video presentation started playing on the screens all around the hall. The video started off with a news clip from CNN, reporting a mysterious outbreak in Eastern Uganda. Then, images of patients—in a makeshift village hospital—exhibiting respiratory and hemorrhagic symptoms soon followed. The image was very grim—patients lay motionless, blood everywhere, waiting for the inevitable. The presentation continued with more news clips, one rapidly followed by another, each one a footage of various other countries reporting a similar outbreak. The quick newsflash culminated in a somber video clip of the head of the WHO, declaring another pandemic—the second one in just under a decade.

Viral: The Rise and Fall of a Nation

The Sorotivirus, a filovirus that includes the likes of Ebola and Marburg viruses, took over the world in late 2028. It causes hemorrhagic fever with a Case Fatality Rate currently estimated at about 56%—a very high rate, considering the CFR for Covid-19 was just around 2-3%. The video presentation continued to show various clips, again in quick succession, on the virus' characteristics and behavior.

By the middle of 2029, more than 25% of the world's population was infected. It was the kind of outbreak we've always feared—one as deadly as Ebola but as contagious as the flu. The video then showed a clip on how the cost of keeping the countries' citizens alive, through supportive care, has brought every government down to its knees.

The presentation turned black momentarily, then changed tones.

The second part started with a Khaleej Times news report of a breakthrough from the Mohammed Bin Rashid Medical Research Institute—an antiviral drug was successfully developed with a 98% success rate in controlling the symptoms of the virus. The antiviral, as part of a supportive care regimen, greatly reduced the CFR of the virus down to 15%. It was still high, but it gave the world the much-needed time to find better ways of combating the virus. The video ended with a voice over from the MC, "Today, we have once again proven the resilience of the human race. And we are proud to be at the center of this breakthrough in the fight for humanity's survival." The lights slowly turn on to the applause from the crowd.

"Ladies and gentlemen, a very good evening to you all." said the MC, now on the podium. "I know you are all eager to hear about the news. So, without further ado, I would like to call on to the stage the person who will tell you about the good news—the brain behind this medical breakthrough, Dr. Asiya Al Alami!"

As she walked towards the podium, the large screens

went live again and started a video presentation about Asiya—her early years in medical school to her graduation from Mohammed Bin Rashid University of Medicine and Health Sciences in 2022.

The presentation continued with clips of her days at Harvard University where she took her PhD in Virology. The video ended with a narration of how Dr. Asiya immediately went back home when the pandemic was declared, to join the brilliant minds at the Mohammed Bin Rashid Medical Research Institute. It was then that she introduced the use of AI to repurpose existing antivirals and vaccines. This led to the rapid development of the antiviral currently in use today.

In the middle of the stage now stood Dr. Asiya, all flushed in the adulation of the crowd. "Thank you!" said Asiya, amid the cheers and applause that filled the hall. A few moments later, she turned on her headset and started presenting.

"As many of you may know, soon after the development of the antiviral, our team embarked on a mission to find a vaccine," she began. Then, with a holographic model that appeared on the stage, she started explaining the mechanism of the virus—how it attaches to a protein and begins to multiply, causing platelet dysfunction. This attachment mechanism became the focus of their research.

She then explained how they adopted a similar model currently on trial for Ebola—the use of small interfering RNAs, small pieces of RNA designed to match specific pieces of the virus' RNA. The goal is to get the virus RNA to stick to the siRNA. Once attached, the virus is no longer capable of creating new particles, thus greatly slowing down replication.

"We were able to create a vaccine that showed promising results in lab testing. This got us all very excited! So, we immediately moved to the next phase—testing on primates," she continued. "Unfortunately, this is when we hit a snag."

She explained that, despite the success in a lab setting, actual testing on primates did not yield a similar result. It was able to inhibit viral reproduction, but it also triggered an aggressive immune response—a cytokine storm that caused rapid deterioration and death of the test subjects.

"We worked on it for days, with little to no sleep," she said. "Then after a number of sequencing, we found what we've been missing—we discovered an unknown strain that we did not notice previously." She posited that it was probably because of the speed at which the virus mutated. With this discovery they theorized that finding the primordial strain might be the key in stabilizing the vaccine.

They sifted through all available data on the initial case reports, until they found the most likely location of the primordial strain—a bat cave in the Maramagambo forest in Bushenyi, Uganda. They set up an expedition team, led by Dr. Praveen, to find and obtain samples.

"Dr. Praveen, please stand up," asked Asiya. A spotlight at the front row pointed to the direction of Dr. Praveen as he stood up. The hall was once again filled with applause from the crowd. "Dr. Praveen and his team's work made this breakthrough possible. They brought home the goods. Thank you doctor," Asiya continued.

"We sequenced the samples from the cave and the strain perfectly matched the unknown strain that we had earlier missed. It was the turning point in our research," she explained further. "From there it was just a matter of synthesizing the proteins and adding them to the formula, and the result was just extraordinary—"

Dr. Asiya took a long pause, looked at the audience, took a deep breath, then with a big smile and visible sparkles in her eyes, she concluded, "Ladies and gentlemen, today we proudly announce—not only have we developed a vaccine—we have developed the cure!"

The hall thundered with applause.

Amid the rumbling noise, Dr. Syeda, the CDPC head and Asiya's mentor in medical school, walked to the podium. "I would like to request Dr. Asiya to please remain on stage as we present her the CDPC Lifetime Achievement Award for her outstanding contribution to medicine," says Dr. Syeda. She then walked towards a visibly surprised Dr. Asiya to hand her the award.

As the evening's affair came to an end, Dr. Syeda approached Asiya and said, "Congratulations, my dear! I always knew you were bound for great things." She then turned to Asiya's parents, shook their hands and congratulated them. She then looked at Asiya and said, "Enjoy the rest of the night. Tomorrow we ship the very first batch of the vaccine."

Asiya left the hall with her parents, award in hand, feeling like a Rockstar. She knew that this was just the beginning. But for now, she allowed herself to bask in her achievement. She is elated, happy, and excited—perhaps way too much that she begins to wonder if she'd be able to catch any sleep before going to work tomorrow.

CHAPTER 3

On the way to the pinned location, Asiya's mind wanders—A secret division? Stem cell agents? Who were those men in black? Her thought was abruptly interrupted.

"Your destination is on the right," says the synthetic voice, as it pulls off by the side of the road.

Asiya looks out the window and sees a massive structure in the background. The building is considered the most beautiful piece of architecture in the world—its skewed toroidal body, clad in shiny metallic panels, adorned with intricate Arabic calligraphy cut-outs all around—shimmers like a newly-polished golden ring in the early morning sun.

"Why are we at the Museum of the Future?" asked a surprised Asiya, who finds Nasir is no longer inside the car.

She immediately hops off. In front of her stood another massive structure—a statue, in the shape of a hand, depicting the famous 'peace sign' of Dubai's ruler. The statue towers above them, with a height about that of five average adults. At the base of the statue Nasir stands. He seems to be surveying it—moving about, running his hand around it, as if in search of something.

The face of Nasir's wristwatch lights up a dreamy blue just as his hand passes over the center part at the back of the statue. They both hear a beep followed by a hissing sound. Suddenly—a secret door opens up—leading to an elevator. Asiya's jaw drops in astonishment. Nasir walks in, turns around, and looks at Asiya.

"The government built a bunker to act as an operations center in the event the protocol was ever activated," he said. "Where better to ensure the continuity of the future than where we celebrate it? Come, follow me."

As the elevator takes them down tens of meters below the surface, Nasir explains, "This is built to withstand all known ballistic missiles, nuclear or otherwise, currently in any nation's arsenal. This is designed to be the command center of the 'Muwaasala Division'—the designated continuity arm of the government. The 'stem cell' agents under it come from various military and civilian disciplines."

The elevator stops and the doors open to reveal the operations center.

The underground bunker is lined with reinforced steel. The main area is a massive square space, enough to fit three commercial airplanes stacked on top of each other. In the center is a circular command—fitted with multiple screens and various devices and implements. At the edge of the main area are multiple entryways, each leading to a tunnel.

All around the operations center, spider-like robots are scattered everywhere—moving about and doing various tasks efficiently and independently. Some were replacing light bulbs, others were painting walls. There were some doing welding jobs while others repair carbon plating on vehicles. She even sees a bunch of them in a far corner, disassembling, cleaning and assembling weapons, then lining them up neatly on racks as they finish.

Inside the circular command center, sits a huge digital round table with a dynamic map overlay. Its size is enough to comfortably sit around 18 adults had it been a dining table. On top floats a holographic image of the city that corresponds to the map underneath it. The hologram shows the buildings damaged from the earlier attacks, the locations affected, the casualties as well as the distribution of first responders, which are spread dangerously thin.

Asiya notices a man approaching from one of the many tunnels that lead to the main bunker area. The man's movements seem calm and collected—chin held high, shoulders back and chest out. He stops in front of them, just opposite the table.

"Hello Asiya," the man says. "Namir, I take it the mission went well?" he said looking at Nasir.

"Yes sir!" Nasir responded with a salute. "The high-value asset was extracted. She has minimal injuries," he continues as he walks towards the man.

"Wait a—are you talking about me? You were sent there for me?" a confused Asiya asked Nasir.

Before Nasir could respond, the man says, "Asiya, come with me. I should be able to clear this all up for you."

Asiya complies.

The man introduces himself to Asiya by his callsign, Saqr. He is the designated Supreme Commander for the Aistimraria Protocol and the head of Military Command of the Muwaasala Division. He oversees the entire operation of the Division, which comprises various commands and departments.

Saqr goes on to explain why Nasir was at the research facility—extracting her is, in fact, Nasir's mission. The vaccine she created is the target of a powerful group, led by a man known to his people as 'Alhami' or 'The Protector'. The Intelligence department got hold of an intel that the group is looking to obtain all information to replicate the vaccine and eliminate all those involved in its creation. "Their goal is simple—complete monopoly of the vaccine for maximum financial gain and political leverage," Saqr explains.

He then breaks the horrific news to Asiya that all her team members involved in the vaccine development have been killed, with the exception of one—Dr. Praveen.

"As we speak, a team of special forces is getting ready for a mission to extract him and take him to safety. I will lead this mission myself," says Saqr.

"Do you have any questions?" Saqr asks.

A voice from behind butts in abruptly, "I have—why are you dumping all this on this poor young woman?"

Asiya turns to the direction of the voice that sounds eerily familiar.

"...Dr. Syeda?" says a shocked Asiya.

"Hello dear," Dr. Syeda responds. "I am the Chief Medical Officer and the head of the Division's Medical Command. They call me 'Maha' around here."

Saqr and Nasir leave quietly to allow Asiya and Maha to catch up. The men move to a briefing room adjacent to the command center to discuss their missions.

"I'm sorry dear, I know there is a lot here to process but we have very little time." Maha says. "I will fill you in once we are done with our missions. But right now, we need to protect the future from this threat, and you have a role to play in this."

"Why me?" she asks.

"There are always two copies of the vaccine data at any given time—one is housed in the research center—the original work—and the other is with the head of MEDCOM—me," Maha explains.

Maha then tells Asiya that a few minutes after she arrived home from that CDPC event last night, a group of men—in black uniform—infiltrated her house. She hid and watched them on the security monitors in her panic room. The men moved to her secret vault without hesitation—as if they knew exactly where to look.

"I was forced to trigger the self-destruct on my copy. It was too late to retrieve it. They torched my whole place to the ground soon as they realized the copy was destroyed," she continues.

"Then, this morning, the attack on the research facility resulted in the destruction of the server that houses all the work in the lab. With the original work and my copy destroyed, the only copy that survives is yours. That is why I need you and Nasir to get it before anyone else does. It's at your house I assume?" Dr. Syeda asks.

Asiya stood there all confused. "What do you mean I have the copy? I am familiar with the strict protocol at work—no information is allowed to leave the lab and I take that seriously. I swear to you I did not bring any work home."

"Forgive me dear, I went ahead of myself," Maha says. "When I was informed of the threat to the vaccine yesterday morning, I implemented the data protection protocol. Before going to the event last night, I downloaded a full copy of the work to an encrypted flash drive. The drive is protected by both our biometrics. That flash drive is inside the award I gave you—hidden within its base."

"My God, it's in my parents' house. I hope they are okay. Please tell me no one else knows about this." Asiya sounded concerned.

"Only you and I know about this. They should be safe," Maha assures Asiya. "I only briefed Saqr just a few minutes before you arrived. So, he's arranged his best men to be your protection detail to ensure your safety. They will escort you to your parents' house. I need you to retrieve the flash drive. Then bring it to a secure location where I will meet you. Nasir will know how to get there. He is being briefed by Saqr as we speak. You should all be leaving soon."

She hugs Asiya. "Please be safe, dear."

"I will. You too," Asiya responds.

The next few minutes pass in a flash for Asiya. The men move around her like a tornado, gearing up for the mission and preparing the armored trucks. She stands there awkwardly, waiting for someone to give her any direction. After a while, a soldier approaches her and guides her to a truck, in the middle of the convoy, with Nasir on the steering wheel. Shortly after all truck doors have slammed shut, the convoy begins to roll.

Asiya sits silently in the passenger seat. In front she counts two matching trucks, and, behind them, another two. Every once in a while, their vehicle's NavSat system gives out prompts to guide Nasir to their destination. They drive along the Jumeirah Beach Road, where a strip of villas partially blocks her view of the beach.

Nasir's radio turns on, "Attention, ETA 10 minutes. Everyone, stay alert." It was a message from the command center, who is monitoring their movement.

Asiya notices the truck at the head of the convoy stop. A tree trunk that fell onto the street blocks their path. "This is Command," the radio chimes in again. "Be advised, we are rerouting your convoy. Your NavSat will show the new route,"

As the two trucks in front of them turn around to follow the new direction, Asiya notices something flashy that went under the first truck—it looks like a smooth, metal sphere about the size of a tennis ball. As Asiya leans in to get a closer look, their truck's engine begins to roar furiously and she feels them suddenly veering away from the convoy. She looks to Nasir, who, at this moment, is in laser-sharp focus. She wanted to ask what that sphere was and what's with the sudden erratic driving. But before she could, she felts a shockwave followed by violent shaking of their vehicle. Then, she sees the first truck in their convoy get flung 10 feet above ground. Nasir steers left and right, trying to regain control of their vehicle and stopping it from flipping over.

As the first truck falls down to the ground, the second truck is sent to the air in similar fashion. Deafening exchange of gunfire breaks out. It is all chaos. The chatter on the comms radio is non-stop. The two trucks that were behind them are almost surrounded by the ambushers. They start firing back with automated turrets, but they could not control the swarm.

Nasir's quick decision-making enabled them to break away in time before the convoy was surrounded. Nasir maneuvers around debris and clutter to get away. Asiya is pushed around her seat, her head connecting with the blunt edge of the window frame a few times.

After a few violent skids and turns the drive smoothes out. Asiya looks back to see the two trucks still fiercely fighting back. She watches in slow motion as two RPGs fire towards the trucks—followed by two massive fireballs shooting up from the RPG's impact site, confirming that the rockets found their intended targets. That was the last scene she saw as they took the corner and lost sight of the battle. The last two trucks fought back valiantly, but failed. They, however, held on long enough to buy Asiya and Nasir time to escape.

CHAPTER 4

Asiya and Nasir stand at the front steps of her parents' home. They move closer to the front door to find it already open. Her heart starts racing. Nasir looks at her and gives out some hand signals—which she was only able to somehow decipher by reading his lips. He signals that they are moving in.

"Oh my God..." Asiya whispers, keeping tears from falling. The place is in chaos— chairs flipped over beneath the kitchen counter to their right, sofa cushions ripped open and thrown to the floor, pieces of shattered glass lay scattered everywhere.

Asiya heads carefully to the cabinet in the corner and sees the award, untouched. It is a silver plaque with a dark wooden ebony base. She picks it up and pries open the base to reveal a thin USB flash drive—their objective. She hands it to Nasir, who puts it in his breast pocket before sweeping the house.

Nasir comes back and tells Asiya all is clear and it is safe to move around.

"Mom?! Dad?!" Asiya calls out shakily—silence. She climbs the stairs to their bedroom. Praying silently and hoping that they would emerge from hiding somehow.

"Mom?! Dad?!" she calls out again as she enters the room. At that moment, she feels her heart drop to the ground—her knees give way and she crumbles to the ground.

There are no signs of her parents. Blood covers the entire room—smears on the walls, stains on the sheets, puddles all over the floor—it's easy to assume the worst. She couldn't bear to look at it anymore, but couldn't take her eyes off it either.

"Namir, this is Command, is the package secure?" Nasir's radio comes to life.

"Affirmative Command." responds Nasir.

"Rendezvous at the meeting point. We have uploaded the location to your NavSat. Be advised, Saqr has been ambushed on their way to their objective. We lost all contact with them. We are still trying to establish comms. Watch your six, agent." The radio went silent again.

Nasir sighs, then kneels down next to Asiya who is still silently sobbing while staring at the ground. He was about to speak out to try and console her when she suddenly stands up, takes a deep breath, and straightens herself up.

"We don't know what happened. This doesn't mean they're gone. They could still be alive," says Asiya. "What are we to do next? Let's keep going," she continues.

They go back to the truck and start heading to the rendezvous point.

Asiya feels numb, unable to feel any emotion. She silently stares out the window for the rest of the ride—she did not even notice when the beach-side view turned into a barren wasteland. Nasir presses a button on the dashboard, and the wheels of the truck adjust their structure to better adapt to the sandy dunes.

CHAPTER 5

Nasir stops the truck, turns it off, and exits the vehicle. They have been on the road for about five hours, but Asiya didn't even notice. Asiya jumps out of the vehicle and follows Nasir like a mindless drone.

She finds herself in the middle of a desert. There are no structures around—just endless undulating dunes in all directions, as far as the eyes can see.

Suddenly, three silhouettes appear from nowhere—just a short distance from where they stand. Asiya looks at Nasir, who doesn't seem concerned. As the silhouettes get closer, Asiya begins to understand why—the men are clad in standard government-issue digital desert camo.

"They're friendly. They're here to meet us," Nasir says to her.

"Nasir!" exclaims one of the soldiers.

"Mohammed? Is that you my friend? How are you?" Nasir asks.

"Yeah, it's me! How long has it been bro, five, six years?" the guy asks.

"Seven years brother!" says Nasir. "How are you?"

"I've seen better days but can't complain. Follow me." the guy says.

They walk towards the spot where they first appeared as silhouettes, then they stop.

"Welcome to Zayed bin Sultan Al Nahyan Base," says another soldier.

Asiya looks confused. There is nothing around but desert. "Have I gone mad?" she mumbles to herself.

She looks closer behind the soldiers, then realizes something, behind them is the blinding desert sun—except, she's not blinded and her eyes could stare directly at it without even squinting. On closer inspection, she notices something else—there are weird streaks in the sky—like tears in the fabric of reality. Unbeknownst to her, Nasir and the soldiers are observing her intently, with grins on their faces, as she tries to understand what she is seeing—or rather—not seeing.

One of the soldiers taps his watch as he looks at Asiya, and right in front of her unblinking eyes appears a massive dome-shaped structure. Suddenly, she could see the sun no more. Her jaw drops completely.

The soldier looks at her, smiles, then says, "Ever seen camouflage, ma'am?"

They all enter the bunker. This one is rather modest—it is still modern by current standards, but is a far cry from the bunker under the museum they visited earlier. They walk down a short tunnel, about 15 meters in length to Asiya's best estimation. Throughout its length were arches, distributed at about every three meters. Each one is about a third of a meter wide—enough to hide a person standing still with his back against the tunnel wall.

At the end of the tunnel, a man, who goes by the codename, 'Ajmal', meets them. He introduces himself to Asiya as the commander of the facility. He appears to be a high-ranking officer, judging by his uniform and his demeanor.

The bunker looks well-equipped. The ceiling is riddled with bright white LED lights that make the inside look more like a high-tech laboratory than a military base.

Computer consoles surround the base. Only a handful of people are there and everyone wears a blue earpiece.

Ajmal hands them the same blue earpieces, along with some food and water. He then begins to debrief them.

"This is one of the most advanced military bases around the world. No other nation has it, and this is one of three we have here in the UAE." says Ajmal. He guides them to the center of the dome, which acts as the command center. By comparison, this is a lot smaller than the one under the Museum of the Future, but this too has a round table fitted with a dynamic map and a holographic overlay. Behind the command center is a heavily fortified room with a wall-to-ceiling bulletproof and explosion-proof glass window, which gives a great vantage point of the entire place.

Ajmal waves his hands around as they stand around the table—he makes various hand gestures until a holographic model of something shaped like an egg appears. He then explains that the dome they saw outside is the top half of a 'subsahra'—a mobile underground base capable of maneuvering under the desert. It is like a submarine for desert.

"You'll be safe here. Maha is en route to meet us, and should arrive very shortly," says Ajmal. "We have also re-established contact with Saqr. He is currently 10 minutes out and is on his way to rendezvous with us. They survived the ambush but they lost a lot of men."

CHAPTER 6

The entrance door to the bunker slides open. From inside, it appears like a big bright ball of light at the end of the tunnel. Through the light appears a silhouette—a shape very familiar to Asiya—a motherly figure that is, unmistakably, Maha.

Asiya begins to walk towards the woman's direction, then says, "Dr. Syeda?"

The silhouette, midway through the tunnel, responds, "Yes Asiya, it is me, child. I am so happy to see you got here sa—" Maha's sentence could not finish and everything that happens next appears in very slow motion—it's as if Asiya is watching an old silent movie with heavily muted sound, except the frames are in full color and each frame lasts a good few seconds.

In front of her, the image of a fallen Maha unfolds—her body, slanted, falling forward on her face. Each successive frame that flashes leaves behind a trail of blood, suspended on air, tracing the path of Maha's fall. As the final frame shows Maha's seemingly lifeless body hit the ground, everything instantaneously goes back to normal speed and Asiya is suddenly overwhelmed by the barrage of sound, the bursts of fire, and the yells and cries all around her. There's gunfire everywhere and Maha is hit—all hell has broken loose.

The sound of soldiers defending the bunker, falling like flies, fills the air.

"Keep formation! Cover right fla—"

"Reloading! Cover m—"

"Maintain your positions! Hold the—"

"No! No! No! No! No!" was all that comes out from Asiya, now tucked on the floor partially behind the cover of a metal desk—knees to her chest, and arms around her legs. Back and forth, she rocks—like a traumatized child, trapped in her own bubble, trying to escape the chaos of the outside world.

Asiya feels a hand grab her arm. She looks up and sees Nasir, who drags her behind full cover. "On my signal, I need you to make a run towards the room in the back. It should be safer there," he says to Asiya.

"Ready!" Nasir fires a volley of suppressive fire. "Go! Go! Go!" he signals Asiya, who immediately obeys. He moves alongside Asiya—his back towards her—while he provides covering fire as they move. They safely get inside the room and Nasir locks the door immediately. His radio beeps and receives word that Saqr is five minutes out. He moves towards the armory, which is inside the room. Asiya on the other hand, finds herself staring through reinforced glass wall, watching the world around her fall apart.

Suddenly, Asiya sees Maha move—weakly, she crawls towards Ajmal's direction. "God, she's alive!" a sense of hope begins to fill her. Then suddenly, she sees Ajmal dash towards Maha, his movements—skillfully sliding from cover to cover, with expert proficiency—bolsters the sense of hope that she begins to feel.

Asiya counts only three defenders remaining—four, including Ajmal. The remaining soldiers are doing their best to keep the attackers at bay. They all seem willing to give up their life to hold the line, until Saqr arrives with reinforcement. They continue to provide cover to Ajmal, who is now almost with Maha.

"Hold the line!" Ajmal screams as he reaches Maha and drags her behind a barrel. He then flings himself behind the same cover. "Damn!" he mumbles to himself—he removes his hand from his abdomen and sees blood gushing—a bullet caught him in that final dash. He tries to apply pressure, but he continues to lose blood. Beside him, a now lifeless Maha lies. A bullet found her during the whole fiasco. He leans to where the barrel meets the tunnel wall and rests his head. He lets out a long sigh, coughs, then closes his eyes.

The eight remaining attackers move surprisingly quickly. They continue to press on, fully intent on breaking the line. Two teams alternate between providing covering fire and pushing forward. At this point, they are now past the position where Maha and Saqr both lie motionless. The attackers, superior in both armor and firepower, continue to pin the defenders—who are now desperately low on ammunition. It is only a matter of time before they are overrun.

Gunfire abruptly ceases—the attackers stop firing. Asiya sees them turn around—like something behind had distracted them. Suddenly, from the tunnel's darkness, a figure emerges behind the attackers—it is Ajmal.

He begins to savagely unload his rifle at the direction of the attackers. Gathering his remaining strength, he makes a final stand. He takes down half of the attackers, and the remaining four are forced to take cover. They are now being hit from two sides.

The attackers sit patiently behind cover while Ajmal continues to fire at them. As soon as the final bullet leaves the barrel of Ajmal's rifle—a solitary bullet, fired from the gun of the attacker's leader, finds Ajmal and deals the final blow.

Ajmal gives out his final order to the men, as he falls, "Hooooold the li—" Then, his body thuds to the ground.

The firefight continues, but is soon interrupted by the

end of the tunnel turning into a big ball of white light once again. Through the light emerges a figure—that of Saqr.

"Yes, Saqr is here!" Asiya says to herself.

The attackers took this disruption as an opportunity to rush the remaining defenders. Saqr races behind the attackers but only gets there just as the last defender drops lifeless on the ground.

"Enough!" says Saqr, with a loud, commanding voice. Everything went silent.

CHAPTER 7

"I did not authorize deadly force against your fellow soldiers!" Asiya hears Saqr say to the attackers, as Saqr's team joins them.

"Sorry sir, we had no choice. They started shooting first," one soldier responds.

It did not take long before Asiya realizes what is going on. Saqr looks in her direction, and walks towards her. She begins to tremble uncontrollably.

Asiya hears beeping from the access panel outside the room. At the same time, Nasir emerges from the armory, in full battle gear—both hands carrying a duffel bag filled with weapons and ammunition. He looks ready to take on a full squad, at the very least, all by himself.

Asiya runs behind Nasir for protection, then the door opens.

Saqr looks at Asiya's direction and says, "Do you have the flash drive?"

"Sir, yes, sir." responds Nasir, much to Asiya's surprise and disgust.

He walks towards Saqr and shows him the drive.

"What the hell is wrong with you!?" she screams at Nasir, who just ignored her. His silence infuriated her even further.

She turns her rage at Saqr, "You! You were entrusted with the responsibility of protecting this nation, and yet, here you are, destroying the very same thing you are meant to protect! You are supposed to protect the people!" Asiya starts crying. "Instead of protecting, you destroy them—those who have dedicated their lives to help build this country!" she said, pointing outside the window. "Those are the people you were supposed to protect! You have a duty—"

An irritated Saqr interrupts her monologue. "Duty?! Do not lecture me about duty, child!" he yells at her. "You have no idea what I've given up in the name of duty!"

"So, what changed? Money? Is that all that's important to you? How did you say it again exactly—maximum financial gain, was it? What kind of man turns his back on his duty and sells his soul for profit? You are disgusting!" says Asiya.

"Profit? Bah! You think I'm doing this for profit?" Saqr scoffed. "I am doing this for the families of my fallen brothers—their wives and their children—innocent people who were left to suffer by the very same government who their loved ones died serving!"

"We started off great as a nation. We performed charity, promoted unity, and practiced tolerance, amongst many other honorable virtues. We stayed true to our constitution—our military was only ever used for national defense, and for humanitarian efforts. I do not know when exactly we lost our way. But, before we knew it, we were being sent to international missions—only this time, it was no longer just for defense or humanitarian aid. I headed a number of those missions myself and, under my command, I watched hundreds of soldiers—fathers, sons, husbands, brothers—lose their lives, for what, for financial and political posturing?" Saqr continues.

"To make things worse, we stopped commemorating our fallen martyrs—with it, the support to the families our martyrs left behind ended," Saqr laments further.

"I can understand if you feel wronged," Asiya says. "But what you're doing is also wrong—and two wrongs don't make one right," she continues. "What you're after is the vaccine—a vaccine that can help save the world. Why deprive the world of this vaccine? This is for humanity!"

Saqr laughs. "For humanity? You think we are doing the world a favor? You think Dr. Syeda is some kind of saint? She is part of the machinery that monetizes this horrific pandemic. Did you really think we plan to give this away for free as some kind of gift to humanity? Yes, we played our part for humanity during the Covid pandemic—but do not, for one second, make the mistake of thinking that we are still that kind of nation. That is long gone and forgotten. Now, it's simply all about who will bid and pay the highest price for the 'commodities' we offer."

"You are too young and too naive to understand, and I would not hold it against you. But, do not ever talk to me about loss or duty! I lost my wife at the beginning of this pandemic. She is a doctor—much like you. When the pandemic struck, she went out of early retirement to serve. The virus took her from me. Then, I lost both my boys to meaningless wars. I dedicated my entire life, and so did my entire family, in service of this nation. Yet, here I am, at the twilight of my life, all alone, with nothing to show for it," reflects Saqr.

"I have nothing else left for me. I no longer have any aspirations for myself. But, I know I can still do something for the ones who were neglected by this government. I have a chance to right the wrongs and get justice for these people—and this is my final mission," says Saqr, who looks at Nasir, and then nods.

Nasir grabs Asiya's right hand, drags her to the glass wall, then cuffs both her hands to the railing. He pulls out a device with a USB port, inserts the flash drive in, and forcibly takes Asiya's thumb to press it against the device.

"Encryption disabled," the device notified. Nasir then puts it back in his breast pocket.

He then walks inside the armory and, and after a few seconds, comes out pushing a trolley—carrying what looks like a bomb on top of it. He presses a button and a 20-minute countdown begins.

Asiya begins panicking, her breaths getting louder and shorter. "Nasir, please, don't do this. Nasir, listen to me. I'm begging you, please. Please!" Asiya wails. Nasir looks at her for a brief moment, then picks up the duffel bags on the floor.

"It is time, son," Saqr says to Nasir, while handing him a pair of keys. He then pulls out a little notebook from his pants' back pocket. "All the information you will ever need is in there. I have made all the necessary arrangements for the transition—you will now answer to the codename 'Saqr' from here onwards. Carry on with our mission, and find a way to mend this nation back to what it once was."

Nasir salutes the man one last time, "Col. Saeed, it was an honor serving with you, sir!" The colonel salutes back. Nasir goes out, locks the door, then heads out and walks towards the bunker exit. The rest of the men followed him. One by one they disappear as they walk into the bright light at the end of the tunnel.

Beep—beep—beep—the clock on the bomb continues counting down. Asiya sits there quietly as she waits out the final five minutes of her life. The old man, Col. Saeed sits on the opposite end of the room, closer to the bomb. He says to Asiya, "Do not worry kid, you will not be alone. I will be here with you when it ends."

Beep–beep–beep–the intervals are now shorter, with just two minutes left on the clock.

The old man begins to speak once again, this time with a much calmer voice—like an old man at the end of his days, sharing the wisdom of his years. Asiya just sits there silently and listens, fully resigned to her fate.

"You may look at me and see an evil villain. But the

real enemy here is the government that has neglected its own people," he begins.

"You see dear child, neglect is a virus that attacks and destroys the very core of any society. Once it has fully infected a society, figuring out where or when it started becomes almost, if not completely, impossible. Without knowing the root cause, we'll never find a real and lasting solution. Every change in administration come with a promise of a solution and a better government. But the end result is always the same—failure—a continuously hemorrhaging nation, endlessly spending on efforts to revive failed or fallen institutions," narrates the man.

"I believe every government gets only one chance at getting it right. We almost did, but something happened along the way, and we blew it," he concludes.

Beep. Beep. Beep. Beep. Beep. The clock now beeps frantically as it counts down the final ten seconds of Asiya's storied, but short existence. The beeping, to her, is now muted—almost inaudible. In total surrender, she closes her eyes as the final beep approaches—then everything goes dark.

CHAPTER 8

Beep-beep-beep! Beep-bee-blag! The beeping is interrupted by a barely awake arm, flailing towards the side table, and hitting the snooze button.

"Good morning, Asiya," greets a synthetic female voice via the bedroom speakers.

"Good morning, Zahira," says Asiya to her trusted home automation AI bot.

Zahira proceeds to her usual morning routine while Asiya tosses and turns in an attempt to shake off sleep.

Zahira: "Based on your sleep patterns and physiological responses, I sense you experienced a sleep disturbance consistent with a nightmare. Your heart rate and breathing rate increased, and your body showed signs of heightened stress while you were asleep."

"Yeah, it was really weird. It felt so real, my heart's still pounding," says Asiya.

Light slowly creeps into the bedroom and the rays of the morning sun begin to gently brush on Asiya's cheeks.

Zahira: "I opened the blinds to let in some morning light. Here is a calming background music to help you settle down."

A gentle strain of classical melody begins to fill the air.

The melody—played softly on a piano—is accompanied by the soothing sounds of a violin and cello. She begins to feel the tightness in her muscles slowly ebbing away—replaced by a sense of peace and serenity.

Zahira: "I started brewing your coffee and have set the shower temperature to your preference. Both should be ready by now."

Asiya is still a little agitated, but Zahira has been a great distraction thus far.

"Thank God it was just a dream," she mutters to herself. She pulls herself up to a sitting position and stares outside the window of her 75th floor apartment in Downtown Dubai. The city's airspace is already buzzing with a number of flying taxis and delivery drones cruising by. Zahira begins a rundown of today's news.

"Today is November 30, 2030. Time is 6:47 am. Here are today's top stories—"

"Khaleej Times— The Emirati-built, 'Humanity Probe' sent to the Main Asteroid Belt in 2028, has just completed its flyby of the dwarf planet, 'Ceres' and is now en route to its target landing site, asteroid 'Pallas'. According to the head of the UAE Space Agency, much like in the Hope Probe's mission, all data collected by Humanity Probe will be made available to the world's scientific community as part of UAE's continuing commitment to distributing knowledge to humanity."

"WAM— The United Nations has commended the UAE for its unwavering commitment to the UN SDG goals. The UAE has achieved an overall performance rating of 85 (out of 100), putting it amongst the Top 10 performers globally."

"The National— The UAE has knocked Finland from the top spot of the Happiest Country in the World ranking."

Asiya stretches, stands up and makes her way downstairs. Near the foot of the stairs, a familiar voice speaks, "Good morning sweetheart! Breakfast is ready."

The man—Asiya's husband, Nasir, in his neatly pressed military uniform—meets her downstairs with a morning kiss. "Slept well?" he asks.

"Dunno. I had the strangest dream!" she responds as she sits at the table. She starts sharing her dream to Nasir, who is busy putting breakfast plates on the table.

After finishing, Nasir sits beside her and assures her that everything is perfectly fine—and that it's all just a dream. The UAE is steadfast in its commitment to providing the best life possible for its people—citizens and residents alike.

"The dream just felt so real," she says. "I can't help but wonder if we'll ever end up in a broken society just like that."

"No one can predict the future," Nasir says. "All we can do is to continue to do good and play our part in nation building, and just hope for the best," he continues. "I am just grateful that our leaders understand the true meaning of leadership—one that serves the people. Governments can put in the strongest, most powerful line of defenses to protect their nation but, much like in your dream, none of those would matter when the most important part of governance is forgotten—the people."

Their discussion is interrupted by a loud slamming of a door. "Mommy...?" says a young boy, about the age of six. He walks towards the dining table as he rubs sleep off his eyes. "Good morning sweetheart," they say to the boy in unison. "Come Yousuf, daddy made us his yummy pancakes," says Asiya.

They finish their breakfast then start getting ready for the day ahead.

"By the way, your parents called while you were asleep. They cannot wait to see you tonight. They'll be there at your awarding ceremony," Nasir says.

Later today, Asiya is receiving an award for her contribution in the development of a drug designed to eradicate Guinea Worm disease and River Blindness.

"Thanks. I will call them on the way to work" says Asiya, as she dresses Yousuf for school. He is extremely excited today because he gets to wear a uniform that matches his dad's. Today is UAE commemoration day—a special day dedicated to honor the country's martyrs and their families.

As they all leave the house to begin their routine weekday journeys, Asiya asks Nasir, "What time are you coming home today?"

"I should be off duty from 3pm. We just need to attend the briefing for the humanitarian mission to Yemen tomorrow, then we're off," he responds. "I'll finish in time to pick up Yousuf from school. We'll go straight home soon after, get dressed, then meet you at the Dubai World Trade Centre for your event later."

They both see Yousuf off to the school bus. Then Nasir climbs into his service Humvee, waves goodbye at Asiya and drives to work. Asiya walks towards the Metro Station, just a few paces away from their building.

Inside the station, she taps her Nol card at the barrier, then heads to the platform. There she finds a train waiting for passengers. She boarded the cabin dedicated for women and children.

She chooses an empty seat by the window, looks outside, then begins to revisit her dream once again. In retrospect, she agrees with Saqr when he likened neglect to a virus—capable of causing widespread havoc and incalculable loss. However, she feels he failed to factor in that viruses mutate and, with it, the host changes too in order to survive. We are a very resilient and adaptable species; highly capable of turning anything negative—like neglect—into a catalyst for change.

The UAE lies in a region that has been neglected by the rest of the world for a good while. But despite the challenges that come with the territory, this nation has risen above and made strides in championing the needs of its people and also that of the world's. Now, it is at the forefront of ushering in a new model of effective and sustainable governance—one that truly is for the people, above all else.

"I can only hope it catches on like a virus and infects the rest of the world." Asiya thinks to herself, as the train begins to move.

ABOUT THE AUTHOR

The son of a Civil Engineer and an English teacher, Dozer Millon Jr. began an early fascination in writing and storytelling. Born in the Philippines in 1979, moved to the Middle East in 1991 and has lived in the UAE since 1995.

Dozer's first work, entitled Viral: The Rise and Fall of a Nation, is inspired by his first-hand experience of living in the UAE and witnessing its development as a nation. It is a fast-paced action thriller that takes readers on a heart-pounding journey through a world of secrets, betrayal, and unexpected twists.

A Civil Engineer by education, a wannabe-but-chose-not-to-be doctor, a tech enthusiast, an avid sportsman, a frustrated musician, an aspiring author, a friend, a son, a brother, a husband and a father, Dozer summarily describes himself as a "Jack of all trades, (hopefully) master of some". You can reach him at
dozermillonjr@gmail.com

Made in the USA
Columbia, SC
17 October 2023